Suddenly You
Hear a Voice!

"You'll never get across unless you ride on my back."

You look down. A huge crocodile is talking to you!

"I'll make a deal with you," the crocodile says. "I'll take you across the river if you will take me back with you to the Enchanted Forest."

If you swing across on a vine, turn to page 16.

If you cross the river on the crocodile's back, turn to page 18.

**WHATEVER YOU DECIDE TO DO,
YOU'RE IN FOR LOTS
OF THRILLS AND ADVENTURE
IN THE EXCITING
ENCHANTED FOREST!**

WHICH WAY SECRET DOOR Books for you to enjoy

Available from ARCHWAY paperbacks

which way·secret door·books

#11

R.G. Austin

The Enchanted Forest

Illustrated by
Winslow Pels

AN ARCHWAY PAPERBACK
Published by POCKET BOOKS • NEW YORK

To Luke, Chris, Larry,
Jessica and Elizabeth with love

AN ARCHWAY PAPERBACK *Original*

An Archway Paperback published by
POCKET BOOKS, a division of Simon & Schuster, Inc.
1230 Avenue of the Americas, New York, N.Y. 10020

ISBN: 0-671-47572-X

First Archway Paperback printing March, 1984

10 9 8 7 6 5 4 3 2

AN ARCHWAY PAPERBACK and colophon are
trademarks of Simon & Schuster, Inc.

WHICH WAY is a registered trademark
of Simon & Schuster, Inc.

SECRET DOOR is a trademark
of Simon & Schuster, Inc.

Printed in the U.S.A.

IL   1+

ATTENTION!

READING A SECRET DOOR BOOK
IS LIKE PLAYING A GAME.

HERE ARE THE RULES

Begin reading on page 1. When you come to a choice, decide what to do and follow the directions. Keep reading and following the directions until you come to an ending. Then go back to the beginning and make new choices.

There are many stories and many endings in this book.

HAVE FUN!

It is dark outside. You have gone to bed, but you are still wide awake.

You lie quietly until everyone in the house is asleep. Then you creep out of bed and tiptoe into the closet.

You push away the clothes and knock three times on the back wall. Soon the secret door begins to move. It opens just wide enough for you to slip through.

Turn to page 3.

Welcome
to the
Enchanted
Forest

There is a sign on the other side of the door: "Welcome to the Enchanted Forest."

You look around. You see beautiful trees and flowers. Birds sing and swoop through the air. You hear music coming from deep in the forest.

You start to walk toward the music. But just then, a tiny red bird lands on your shoulder.

"Come with me and I will show you the secret of the Enchanted Forest," says the bird.

If you want to go with the bird, turn to page 4.

If you would rather go to the music, turn to page 7.

"Is this forest really enchanted?" you ask the bird as you walk.

"It sure is," the bird says. "Look! The hawk and the mouse are playing tag together; the lion and the lamb are playing hide and seek!"

"What causes the enchantment?" you ask.

"The magic crystal," the bird says. "It's right over there."

The bird points its wing.

"I don't see any crystal," you say.

"Oh, no! It's been stolen!" the bird cries.

"We'd better get to Genie fast. If we don't get the crystal back by sundown, the enchantment will disappear!"

Turn to page 8.

You walk deeper and deeper into the forest. As you walk, the music grows louder.

Then, suddenly, you see a strange instrument hanging from the branch of a tree.

Every time the wind blows, the instrument plays music.

You reach up and touch it. The music stops.

Then you hear a grand roar. "Who dares touch my harp?" says a voice.

If you answer the question, turn to page 12.

If you think the best thing to do is to get away fast, turn to page 15.

You follow the bird to a big oak tree. He points to a lamp hidden in a hole near the roots.

You pick up the lamp. Suddenly, a strange creature rises out of the lamp.

"Please, help us," the bird says to Genie. "The crystal has been stolen!"

"The only one who would do such a terrible thing is Harold," Genie says. "You must talk to him."

"But he lives outside the forest!" the bird cries. "We are forbidden to leave our home."

"I can leave the forest," you say. "Why don't I go talk to Harold?"

"Harold is a terrible monster," says Genie. "And in order to reach his land, you must cross the Crocodile River."

Continued on page 10.

"I have to try," you say. "Otherwise the forest will lose its magic."

"Well, OK," Genie says. "But take this magic ring. If you rub it and make a wish, your wish will come true. But you have only one wish, so use it wisely."

When you reach the Crocodile River, you see long vines hanging from the trees. The water is filled with crocodiles.

Suddenly you hear a voice.

"You'll never get across unless you ride on my back."

You look down. A huge crocodile is talking to you!

"I'll make a deal with you," the crocodile says. "I'll take you across the river if you will take me back with you to the Enchanted Forest."

If you swing across on a vine, turn to page 16.

If you cross the river on the crocodile's back, turn to page 18.

If you want to play it safe and use your wish to get across the river, turn to page 20.

"It's only me," you say. "I didn't mean to hurt anything."

"But you stopped my music!" the voice says. "No one stops the music of the Wind!"

You look around, but you do not see anyone.

Suddenly a huge gust sweeps

you off the ground. You grab hold of a branch just in time.

"You are banished to the Garden of the Golden Apples. There, you will have to fight Ladon, the dragon."

"I won't go," you say.

"You have no choice," says the wind.

Turn to page 24.

You start to run. Faster and faster you run through the Enchanted Forest.

Oops! You trip and fall.

Ouch! You have sprained your ankle.

If you break a branch off a tree so you can use it as a crutch, turn to page 29.

If you sit there awhile and hope someone will come along to help you, turn to page 35.

You grab the end of one of the vines and move away from the river. Then you take a running start.

Wheeee! You swing right over the crocodiles.

Oh, no! You forgot to let go and you're back over the river again!

Back and forth! Back and forth! You pump with your whole body.

Then you let go!

Thump! You just make it.

You stand up and look around. At the top of a hill you see a bright, sparkling glow.

You run up the hill. When you get to the top, you discover a whole cave filled with crystals.

"Hooray!" you shout. "I've found the crystal!"

"Nonsense!" says a deep voice. "There are many crystals here. And only one is enchanted! The others are plastic!"

You look up. You are staring right into the crazy eyes of a gigantic fly.

Turn to page 23.

Nervously, you climb onto the crocodile's back. You hang on tightly as he slithers into the water.

"All right, all right, move it!" the crocodile yells as he swims through a crowd of his friends.

You are so scared that you cannot stop shaking.

Finally, you reach the other side of the river.

"The crystal is in that cave up there," the crocodile says, pointing to the top of a steep

hill. "But you're going to have a tough time finding it. The cave is filled with phony plastic crystals. Only one of them is the real thing. And watch out for Harold. He guards the cave. He's big and mean and ugly."

Turn to page 46.

"I wish I were on the other side of the river," you say as you rub your ring.

WHOOSH! You are on the other side of the river.

Oops! You have landed right on top of a very cranky crocodile.

And you have used up your wish.

Too bad!

The End

"You'll never find the enchanted crystal," says the fly, laughing. "Go ahead and look. If you find it, you can have it. But, if you don't, I shall imprison you in the middle of one of the plastic crystals. You'll look just like a bug in an ice cube."

You shudder at the thought.

If you want to use your wish now, turn to page 26.

If you try to locate the enchanted crystal without using up your wish, turn to page 44.

Suddenly the angry wind lifts you into the air.

You begin to spin. Faster and faster you spin. When you stop, you are standing near a walled garden.

Tree branches, filled with golden apples, hang over the top of the wall.

Oh, boy! you think. *I sure would like to take some of those apples home with me!*

Suddenly you hear a growling roar. You turn around. There is a huge dragon racing toward you!

If you try to run from Ladon, turn to page 30.

If you try to climb the wall, turn to page 32.

You rub your ring.

"I wish I could find the crystal right this very minute," you say.

In an instant, you are standing next to the enchanted crystal.

"I have it!" you exclaim as you bend over to pick it up.

Ugh! You cannot lift it. It is too heavy.

And you have no more wishes!

The End

You pull yourself up and snap off a branch.

Suddenly you are grabbed from behind. You turn and see a strange and beautiful creature. And you smell a very yucky smell.

"Leave me alone!" you cry.

"Alone alone alone," says the woman.

"What do you want?" you ask.

"Want want want."

She pulls you toward a giant pine tree. At the bottom of the tree, you see several tiny creatures. The stinky smell is even stronger now. You hold your nose.

"Who are you? Why did you drag me here?" you ask.

"We are Wood Nymphs," answers a young man. "Echo, the nymph who brought you here, caught you breaking one of our trees. You must be punished!"

Turn to page 36.

You run toward the gate as fast as you can. Ladon runs after you.

Yikes! you think. *He's getting closer!*

You are not sure you're going to make it. You are almost to the gate. Here comes Ladon!

Oops! You lose.

Ladon has a new playmate.

The End

Luckily, the wall is made of old bricks. Some of them have fallen out. You find a toehold and then a handhold. And then another and another.

Ladon is close! You can feel the heat of his breath. Quickly you grip a brick at the top and pull your body over the wall.

You made it!

The inside of the garden is beautiful. Golden apples hang from the branches of the trees.

You pluck an apple.

I have two hands, you think. *I can take two apples. But if I do, I won't have a free hand to use if I need it.*

If you take two apples, turn to page 39.

If you take one apple, turn to page 40.

You sit there and rub your ankle. You try to stand up.

Ouch! It hurts to walk. You sit back down.

Well, you think. *This is pretty stupid. In fact, this is a very stupid adventure. I don't like this place at all! Phooey on Enchanted Forests! I hate trees! I hate this! I wish I were home!*

And that's exactly where you are. There is no more enchantment, no more magic, no more adventure—unless you begin again.

The End

"But I sprained my ankle and needed a crutch," you say.

"That is a good reason for breaking the branch," the nymph says. "If you can help us, we will not punish you."

"How can I help you?" you ask.

"The River Nymphs are angry because we built a dam in their river to make a swimming pool. Now they won't even let us take baths in the river. We even took the dam down, but they still won't let us bathe. We're beginning to stink."

If you talk to the River Nymphs and try to convince them to change their minds, turn to page 42.

If you try to trick the River Nymphs, turn to page 48.

You take an apple in each hand and walk out the gate.

I'm safe, you think.

Then suddenly, you hear a roar! Ladon was hiding!

Look out! He's coming for you!

You run.

Ladon spits fire at you!

You turn and fling an apple right at his fiery snout. The apple hits the dragon! He is furious!

Then the apple melts from the heat. The melted gold drips all over Ladon's face. He stops and paws at the dripping gold.

And you run all the way home . . . with your golden apple.

The End

You take one apple and run out of the garden.

"Grrrooooarrrrr!" the dragon yells when he sees you.

He runs toward you, spitting fire.

Uh-oh, you think. *I'd better give him back his apple!*

You drop the apple and keep on running. The dragon stops and picks up the apple.

You are free!

That's probably the only time in my life I'll ever be saved by a golden apple! you think.

The End

You walk to the river. "Hey! River Nymphs!" you yell.

A tiny head pops out of the water. "Are you a friend of the Wood Nymphs?" the little nymph asks.

"Yes, but—"

"Well, we won't talk to you!"

Well, you think, *I gave it a try.*

You walk back to the Wood Nymphs and whisper to them. They start to giggle.

Then you all walk back to the river. One by one, the Wood Nymphs talk to the trees. Slowly, the trees begin to walk away from the bank of the river. Soon, there are no more trees.

Turn to page 50.

Plastic crystals, you think. *That's very interesting.*

You tap one crystal with a stone. Thud. It makes a very dull noise.

That one must be plastic, you think.

One after the other, you tap the crystals with your stone.

Thud, thud, thud! Thud, thud, thud, thud!

You keep on tapping.

Thud, thud, thud, thud. Thud, thud, thud, thud, thud, thud, ding!

Ding? you think.

You tap again. *Ding!*

This is the magic crystal! you think.

You try to pick it up. It's too heavy to lift.

I'm glad I saved my wish till now, you think.

You rub your ring.

"I wish to return to the Enchanted Forest with the magic crystal," you say.

"No sooner said than done," says the voice of Genie. "After all, a hero deserves quick service!"

The End

You start to climb up to the cave. The mountain is steep and . . . OOPS!

"Yikes!" you yell as you slide right toward the edge of a cliff.

You grab hold of a branch just as you are about to go over the edge.

That was a close call, you think as you start to climb again. Finally, you get to the cave.

But there is a gigantic fly guarding the entrance.

I'm going to have to figure out a way to get past that monster, you think.

If you try to flatter Harold so he will let you in the cave, turn to page 52.

If you try to play it cool, turn to page 54.

"I've got an idea," you say.

"Tell us!"

Soon all the Wood Nymphs are running and playing and sweating. Then they roll around in the dirt.

Before long they are very dirty and very *very* smelly.

Then all the Wood Nymphs walk down to the river and sit along the banks.

Pretty soon you hear the River Nymphs talking.

"P.U. What's that awful smell?" says one as she holds her nose.

"Sure does stink around here," says another.

"Oh, no!" says a third. "It's the Wood Nymphs!"

You hear whispering. Then one of the River Nymphs comes out of the water. "All right," she says. "You may take baths. But only on one condition."

"What is it?" the Wood Nymphs ask.

"That you do it RIGHT NOW!"

The End

You sit by the river and wait. Soon you hear voices.

"Hey!" says one. "It's hot in here!"

"Wow!" says another. "I'm boiling."

"I feel like I'm living in a bath tub!" says a third.

"If I liked this kind of weather, I would have become a Desert Nymph! This is a drag!"

"Hey!" calls one of the River Nymphs. "If we let you bathe, will you give us back our shade?"

"Sure!" the Wood Nymphs yell as they dive into the water.

The End

"Wow!" you say as you walk over to the ugly fly. "You sure are handsome! I've never seen a monster as good-looking as you."

"Handsome? Good-looking?" the fly says. "I'm ugly. Everyone says so."

"Ugly? How silly! Look at those long hairy legs and those big sparkling bug eyes. And

your wings? Like dew drops on
a summer morning! You're gorgeous!
Haven't you ever seen yourself?"

"No," the fly says. "I haven't."

"Well, why don't you look at yourself in a
crystal?" you ask.

"There's only one real crystal in here,"
says the fly. "Let's see . . . which one is it? Oh,
yes. Here it is! It's too dark in here," the fly
complains. "I can't see myself."

"Then why don't you go down to the river
and look in the water?" you suggest.

While the fly buzzes down to the river, you
rub your ring.

"Quick!" you whisper. "Get me and the
crystal back to the Enchanted Forest!"

"You got it!" says Genie's voice. "You're
one smart kid!"

The End

"Hi," you say to the fly. "How's it going?"

"Aren't you scared of me?" the fly asks.

"Why?" you ask. "You're nothing special."

"Oh, yes I am. I am ugly! I am weird! I am scary! I am special!"

Suddenly you get an idea.

"You're no more special than all those silly crystals in that cave," you say. "They're all the same."

"Aha!" says the fly. "You're wrong! One of those crystals is *very* special . . . just like me."

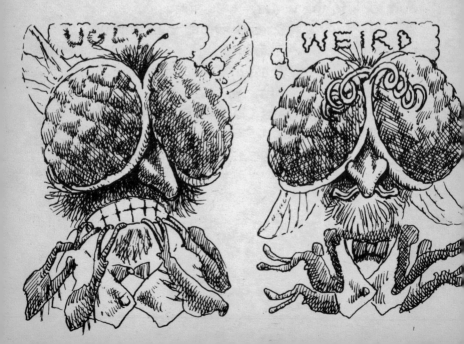

"I don't believe you. Show me!" you say.

"It's that one right there!" the fly says, pointing. "That one is different. It's magic!"

"Nooooo," you say.

"Yes, it is," the fly says. "If I take it back to where it came from, everyone will celebrate."

"No way!" you say. "I don't believe you."

"I'll prove it," says the fly. He picks up the crystal. "Meet me in the forest. Then you'll see I'm telling the truth!"

Continued on page 56.

Quickly you run down the hill.

"Come on!" you say to the crocodile. "Let's get to the forest!"

When you arrive, the entire forest is celebrating. And you are given a hero's welcome!

You look around and see the fly in a huge cage. When the monster sees you, he waves his wing. "See?" he says. "There *is* a celebration. I told you so!"

"You're right," you say happily. "I believe you now."

The End